By Dawn's Early Light

at 120 Miles per Hour

Roger Aplon

Dryad Press

San Francisco
Washington, D.C.

1983

Some of these poems have previously appeared in the anthology
The Young American Poets and the following magazines:
Suisun Valley College Review, Look Quick, F1, Choice, Eleven.

Cover photo: Gus Foster *Six Seconds Real Time*
(Detail) 1440° Panorama
Cover design by Gus Foster and Janet Webb

This project is supported by a grant from the
National Endowment for the Arts, a Federal agency.

LIBRARY OF CONGRESS CATALOGING IN PUBLICATION DATA

Aplon, Roger, 1937-
  By dawn's early light

  I. Title.
PS3551.P45B9   1983   811'.54   83-1840
ISBN 0-931848-58-X
ISBN 0-931848-57-1 (pbk.)

Dryad Press

Presidio P. O. Box 29161
San Francisco, CA 94129

15 Sherman Avenue
Takoma Park, MD 20912

CONTENTS

for Jason

STARTING OVER

for Levinia

I lay in the weeds
at the side of the road
capping the snapped veins
with my hands
hugging the shredded skin
around the muscle
cushioning my bones.

Will I wear a sling, a brace
stumble around on crutches
crawl?

Will these small black ants
burrowing higher
as the water rises
find my eyes
will the trackers come
search in the rain?

Weeks go on
the healing begins
I learn to suckle the warm sheep
eat grass
inch along, only
an occasional shudder now
when the slivers of glass
swim up the puckered skin
that will be the scars.

I

DESERT LANDSCAPES

WHEN INTEREST IS HIGH
for Brenda Hyde

"there is some s.   I will not eat"
                c.c.cummings: i sing of Olaf glad and big

When interest is high
everything must be eaten
      quickly:

platters of buttered potatoes, cabbage soup,
beef smothered in sautéed onions
bowl after bowl
capped in layers of ripe gruyere.

When interest is high,
everything rich must be eaten.

Inside this bakery,
inside these loaves on trays,
the once juicy
berries of wheat
      revive!
Ovens burst:
wave after wave of grain
and no one fit to feed . . .

•••••

This October afternoon is still,
only an occasional puff
to wag the flag.
The railing of the bridge is hot,
unseasonal.

Her skirt's too tight,
the height jarring.

13

My interest is high, she says,
my time to fly . . .
At these moments
rescue wants a favor:
I'll take a tailored worsted
skirt too tight
one leg up—one leg not.

•••••

In the coal camps of northern Kentucky
tall wiry men and lean women
learn to use their new (government issue)
indoor toilet.
They call their children inside and shit,
wipe their buns in unison, flush and applaud.
The entire family applauds.
There is *great* interest here.

•••••

Interest *is* important.

On a diet?
         Try a sandwich!

He eats the meat
                between the buns
hums to himself
smacking those interested lips
admiring his technique—his
        efficiency
dazzling her disinterested mirror—her
                  cat
    her
two
    tongue wagging spaniels
all this quaint mènage.

•••••

And as interest grows higher, you remember again
your uncle Max
tipping his last pint of Guinness stout and pointing
    to the scarred cash box
tacked to the foot of his bed
its smashed lid purporting violence and a fortune won.

Today you flushed your last grouse
missing badly.

Today you sent *your* nephew
running to change
your combinations
and called
too late
your broker
who could move you into deeds.

"Interest up or interest down"
can't check that croak in your flabby throat.

•••••

Yes, when interest is high
advantage
        eats
            willfully. No,
not like my friend Sid
emaciated in death
hugging his interest,
his small pouch
stuffed to the top:
the dried eyes
of his Korean kills.

•••••

The oyster shucker knows best:
to enhance interest
ignore the sand
call it texture
suck down the juice
chew the body
never
      just
          swallow
               it
                  whole.

•••••

And . . . even if your interest is high
don't butcher your neighbors for blood,
(this scene makes my mother sick).
She learned to enjoy high interest.
She learned it from Dad.
Dad has chosen to ignore neighbors
                      who butcher
          each other
for blood.

•••••

Seafood (when interest is up) is best,
no blood here,
                (tuna excepted),
filet the catch,
                (I prefer Red Snapper),
build the baker this way:
   one layer thin sliced white onions
   one layer thin sliced tomatoes
   one layer fish filets
   one layer sliced lemons.

Over all scatter:
parsley-chopped
garlic-sliced
jalapeños-diced
butter
salt and pepper.

Douse liberally with dry white wine and bake at 350 degrees
for 20 minutes or until the flesh is tender and flakes easily.

Remove filets to serving platter, decorate with vegetables
and sauce from the pan.

Eat it all!
Keep *your* interest high.

TRAILING THE ARMY

There are armies
crossing Nebraska.
Armies that fatten on leftover cows
armies so silent and sure
they lumber over the day
unmindful of sweat
forgetting rivers
crossed and recrossed.
I am trailing the army
gouging huge holes in their water bags
clipping the sharp eyes of their bayonets
exhausting their mothers with stories
of past atrocities.
Someone has to follow.
Someone must nip at the wide black haunch.
They are well organized and have learned
the rewards of cutting
everything down.
Everything that grows on its own
is suspect.
No one has survived the wave on wave
of their perfect form.
Even the frogs
fall game.
The nights are filled with their music;
They mimic the chords and pipes of human throats.
In Kansas City there are people
already overcome.
In St. Louis there are people of knowledge
catching planes.
In Detroit
no one has even begun to care.

"Some Kids Set Me On Fire. They Poured Kerosene On Me From a Milk Container and Lit Me With Matches"

The sky's collapsed.
White mice in blown glass
pack oranges
sucking lethal baskets of yarn.
They run under the exhilaration of death
feet sizzling
through rivers of rain.
Their nails nip the cement
in a tattoo of tiny rockets.
The air's liquid with lettuce
and an avalanche of laughing eyes.
At the end of Avenue B
hovering in the roots of old hands
a stink of furious fingers
soundlessly
gagging.

OCTOBER 9, 1967

for Che Guervara

The toads sing at sundown
long, rhythmic chants
like the clapping of shoes.

Hoot owls light the sky.
Roosters molt in the jack-pine
turning blue.

I camp in the snail's track. Small
veiled girls seranade my night,
their soft bones turned
fodder for the goats.

The mountains are hardest
trails like polished eyes.

I slake my thirst on the lips of tigers,
rest in the throats of hummingbirds.

                                    In La Paz
I sell my teeth for beetle's wings, trade
radios for gunpowder,
assemble bombs.

I visit Beirut.
400 Moslems shit and belch-up fisheyes;
in Terre Haute they crush my hands,
castrate the horse,
flog my mole til his asshole pops;
Dallas buries my tongue,
hangs my skull in dormitory windows.

20

I keep to the backroads.
My eyes leave a slick trail on your bedroom doors.
Your plumbing's jammed with my clenched fist.
I'm under your collar
burrowing along your spine.

IN THE MOUNTAINS

the boar's fur is beginning to mat
rainbow trout school under the falls
armies of black ants haul their eggs from one hill to another
girls w/blue knapsacks hitch-hike to Oregon
friends give each other everything they own
in the night
whole suburban towns have been evacuated and hidden
somewhere in the Gulf of Mexico

DESERT LANDSCAPE: ROOTS CLOUDS AND WATER

"It works. . . . It's beautiful!"
J. Robert Oppenheimer
Alamagordo, New Mexico
7/16/45

1.

At first
there are just
his tumescent roots
flat
 grey
  enamel

working up and out
even as we talk
the muck
clay makes
of inland lakes.

Their soaring turns
this quaint
provincial scene
cacophonous:
   an alarm
  racing
bank
 to
  bank,
concentric whorls of water
its entire
  mile wide
    breath
no feeding fish could make.

•••••

To our left,
all black and blue-lined,
his suspicious columns:
a way out?
Maps to something buried in flight? An undulating
distraction? Wait!
Someone is already ascending.

One tentative hand,
a foot
          another
                      hand . . . So,
He's left a cleft,
chink in the rock, a ladder? . . . Rooms?

2.

Ten of us, at least,
are already lost.
More and more choose the lake.
Sprinting,
they crash together,
driven to grip
their own exceptional
burgeoning
root.

•••••

His landscape has begun to glow:
a yellow juice
oozes over the banks.

The tendrils still
muscle up
slowed only slightly
under their new weight of bone.

They twist sluggishly
then gain height — soon
are lost to grey.
No one has thought to let go.

•••••

Skin and root
a faint memory now
married with lake
with clouds
with tower
slim slip of sky
these faceless acres of sand.

(*After a painting by Rick DeMont*)

II

I FASHION OARS

MIDWESTERN CHRISTMAS
for Marvin

The boy in the blue snowsuit is fat,
nearsighted and snivels
when the whip
snaps back
the snow.
His hands are fans:
bruised blue coral
humming
in the corners
of his elastic mittens.
He's mumbling to himself
stumbling in the slush
one foot in
one foot out.
At the pond
he stops,
cackles at the ducks
growing drunk in the ice.
He thinks
how big he will grow:
Big as the trucks
that haul the hogs away;
Big and bland
as these sloping plains
murmuring to themselves
their own private song.
So he slides along
the surface
of this frozen lake
taking stock—counting
the years ahead,
swallowing the days
one after another,
growing
and planning
his own secret home
under acres of this midwestern snow.

DAUGHTER'S LAMENT

for Ramona

It's Sunday
the 21st of March
two days before my birthday.
I'm hunched on an oak bench
elbows on the kitchen table
chewing my fingers raw.

It's an act I've mastered over the years
my private devastation.

Ma is stirring the pot
her big arms
leaning into the weight
of her long black spoon
plowing the chunks of lamb
celery corn and beans
that churn the soup to stew.

The afternoon light
follows the tips of my naked hands
where they illuminate the wood
like fish, like sunning snakes,
birds . . .
When I touch the buttons at my neck
they turn to gold.
When I move my wrists
there's the music
noble metals make.

I hear the hissing of the beans
bigger and more bouyant
with each turn of the spoon.
Watch her muscled arms
thicken the still air.

Tomorrow I will leave.

I'M THE SPIDER

stringing nets across your door,
a flounder
sucking the waves with one good eye.
I'm desire nursing your tongue,
a hive of stars
blinking answers in the pockets of old men.
I'm the ruin of dogs
            shorn
        and weak
the plotter of crimes —
burglars worship my lips,
rapists smuggle maps in my bottle of thumbs.
I climb blood,
my quill in your heart.
I eat the drops that surface in your fragile cup.

RASSLIN

for Neil Lehrman

Jus in case I didn mention
I'm from Florida
home a the Seminole—mostly
bullshit
an gators . . .

You drive the swamp—see big boards advertisin
the prime bouts
it's the fack
celbrates these parts—
Rasslin Gators

a one time thrill—no shit
got dudes in town
walkin roun
in half their skin
beats cockfights n bullfights all t'hell . . .

Well, I'm gonna do this tune bout rasslin gators—cep
that alays minds me of another story bout
bein back home fur the cure
drugs n all *that shit*—I'm
in this center see
where this dude
jacks off every mornin bout 5 am
wakes the whole damn place
humpin and hollerin
like he's possessed
I swear t'Christ
he never even used his hands
jus humped the goddamn bed
rubbin right through the sheets
like none a us was even there—

I don put down jackin off, fack
I wish we's all that free—no
it's that noise, all that thrashin round—almost like he's
pained ur scared—yeah—like—you got it—like rasslin
like *rasslin gators*

(After a performance by Sandy Bull 5/20/76)

BARSCAPES: THE PHOTOGRAPHER:

It's still
cockcrow
down the rabbit hole.
Who will you trust ?
Mole leads the way.

•••••

The puppeteer's stuttering lids
truss-up his eyes:

my hammer has dazzled the dowagers of Danville
my adze delights the svelte ankles that dangle from telephones
*   in Tucson*
my pliers pull the barrels of Butte together

•••••

We'll wait till 4 am,
play croquet,
demand Sunnybrook for lunch,
disintegrate in sautéed onions,
be reborn
at mother's teat. And—
here's where I plan your demise—
can keep you forever . . .

I've slept in the cornerstones of enormous iron buildings,
tucked burrs under the saddles of bank examiners.
I revel in my greed,
prefer anonymity,
my hat is my trademark,
the obvious is always the best disguise.

HANDS UP ! gottcha . . . !
•••••

Give us that indelible taste,
that 11 am
bracer, that trip—
hammer 'fall of the die',
lockturned, door-a-jar, kind of in-
quisition, that . . .

The war is here
all around us.
Your lens turns them on.
They hop—grin—puke !

•••••

You're outside
flagging down greyhounds, gulls
and tipsy tricksters . . .

Under the covers
Chris croons to Clarissa,
"Come to my corral, cradle my crazy
crown in your cooing
crotch—Oh! Clutch me to your crutch, Oh!
Count Me In!"

And here my joke dissolves:

'T's born in a 'jar-a-moon'
I'll swill it til I'm still."

(after a photograph by Ramon Muxter)

BARSCAPES: THE BARTENDER

Bloodybull for breakfast
turns over
fast.

Squeeze out the air:
piss, beer, smoke, sweat, dung and fly's eyes . . .

Head tucked in fringed cushions
last night's mamma snores it off —
     I square off
  wipe the oily oak
rag after rag.

Downstairs
Big Jack turns up the soup
knocks back an Ancient Age
mops.

It's been two days since Sunday
the Desoxyn's gone:
I squint through the cellophane curtains,
rub my eyes,
fill the juice tins, ice bins, creamers, coffee pots —
cut fruit as my bowels boil

The air's the same
open the doors
mamma's gone
bank's out
20¢ short
soup's hot
Carrie's scrubbed the tables

last Camel
make it to the can
first shit
flushed
skin grey

Tomato juice—raw egg—Vit. C + B—Milk
11 am

right on time!

(after a photograph by Ramon Muxter)

TAOS, NEW MEXICO: THE FLOOD

for Janet Cannon

Wherever the Rio Grande peaks
its ribs break away.
Acres of clay
careen the rapids
where they stop
a new continent begins.

• • • • •

I fashion oars
stash a sharp ax
bedroll   water
tent and jerky.
I pack the books that tell the habits of the ocean fish
recipes for kelp.

The earth dissolves.
The river bends.

Add:
one life jacket
lines and hooks
Jason's notes on survival
matches   compass   knife
bandages   iodine
guns and plenty of rounds.

• • • • •

The priests lead their flocks to higher ground.
They are good climbers
and considerate
of the fallen:
many bodies
bolstered on the backs of the strong, young clerics. Soon

they are just a thread on the dim hill
climbing lustfully.

•••••

The bats
unhinge their wings
can only beat the sky
blindly
grope for balance
as the tumult grows.

The owls
still huddle together
the glow from their patient eyes
bright enough
to light the limbs
where they perch
at peace with the dark.

•••••

No time left
for the moon
to slow the tide
I unlash the tiller
and cut the raft away.

Running free
on the crest of the ebb
blind from salt
and deaf
to the clash of land and water
I set the oars deep
and feel the bow
headed true and away
closer with each stroke
to my next berth
on the fringe of this foreign sea.

THE ARSONIST

So, that October night
I burned the lot. Harry
roasted ribs over your underwear,
squeezed sterno through your pale blue peignoir.
The silver brooch with the fucking horses
scorched sea-green, books by Potter
toasted brown as bees. I saved
the bindle of Caine
and an ounce of Thai weed
(smoked it with the crew from engine 5). Stoned
and waving a hose around the edge,
I thought I saw your face
giggling in the bubbling tar,
your arms
stuffed with pillows and fake amber beads.
If you're ever back in town,
Germaine's got your jade earrings
and the locket with cuttings of our pubic hair, be sure
to look me up
I'm generally listed.

III

ENIGMA VARIATIONS

ENIGMA VARIATIONS

for Larry Bell and Ken Price

My friend climbs inside his enormous machine,
$\qquad\qquad\qquad$ locks the lid,
$\qquad\qquad$ tunes the secret knobs,
$\qquad\quad$ and knifing back
$\qquad$ takes himself
to vapor . . . ochre and blue
$\quad$ shadows
$\qquad\qquad$ careening
$\qquad\qquad\qquad$ armpit to crotch.

It's never long:
after the wolves are tamed,
sheep bred—new
seed tossed—
$\qquad\quad$ he returns
tattooed
$\qquad$ and glowing—his
$\qquad\qquad\qquad$ electric fur
$\qquad$ dancing
$\qquad\qquad$ up and over
each filament of sinew
$\qquad\qquad\qquad$ each
$\qquad\qquad\qquad\quad$ muscled eye.

He says, "it feels good,"
and we agree
applauding
$\qquad$ in particular
the plum and coral dolphin as she
$\qquad\qquad\qquad\qquad\qquad$ soars
from the palm
$\qquad\qquad$ of his extended
$\qquad\qquad\qquad$ hand.

•••••

This friend lives in a cup.
Oh! He used to live in pots
                          til cups.
These days the cup is one inch high and one inch
                                        across.

As it warms
the seductive odor of fermenting grain
eases from the top,
permeates the air,
                the ground
                          in all directions . . . hovering.

Inside
            on the upper level
beside the stoves and sinks
the most exotic bebop discs
                ever claimed
        by any cup
of any size.

At the base
a maze of passageways
lures us further back:
to shark
          to turtle
                    the first birds.

Iron, copper and gold tailings
crust the walls and floors:
he's driven deep
resurrecting
one by one
the lives
of these rooms.

A low chant begins close by,
a woven curtain parts,
we are invited in . . .

I'VE SEEN IT AGAIN

for Denny Zeitlin

your absolute hand
raking the tin leaves
of the little african
finger piano
while your other
strides the Steinway
toward some complete
harmonic feat.
And I distinctly hear your foot
stomping its own
accompaniment
as if you were
running in place
far ahead.

NIGHT COMES QUICK IN THE MOUNTAINS

Sheep crowd
      the bush
their little bells
      muffled.
A snake
      the coral of cantelope
eases back
      under the stubble
a light rain
      falling in his violet eye.
Your fingers
      pick the skin
from the peach
      you've caught
scratch my name
      for the crickets
where the trees
      snare them
in the folds
      of their enormous
bark.

THE DANCE

for Ricardo Jimeno Rebollo

The
 snakes
  worked
   their
     way
      a
       cross
         his
           back
         like
       an
      ex
     tra
    lay
   er
  of
 mus
   cle
     rip
       pling
         with
          each
            note
          of
          the
          flute
       as he
breathed
      he was
         ringed
            with
              snakes

when
he
moved
their
eye
lids
quiv
ered
their
teeth
made
the
sound
of
a
claw
and
when
he
stopped
we heard
the
moan
ing
of
the
dew
—then somebody
coughed
and
an
other
got
up

49

to
take
a
leak
he
started
to
play
and
the
moon
went
high
er
and
the
chick
in
the
cargo
net
began
to
dance
with
a
frog
on
the
tip
of
her
tongue
and
Frank

grabbed
his
duffle
and
made
for
the
trees
while
I
knew
the
pur
ple
th
read
that
inched
its
way
a
cross
my
hand
where
it
lay
in
my
lap
was
a
live.

(After Tobias Schneebaum's book Keep the River on Your Right and Rousseau's painting "Snake Charmer")

RED ANTS

nibble the skin of the fox
coaxing a meal.
It's winter.
The Panda
squirms in his bath
sorting rubies
round as duck's eyes.
Under the snow
a black bear
dreams of stuffing his jaws with rainbow trout
as thick as tongue
as slippery as buttered ivory.

PLANTING

Even after
the skin is broken
there's much to do:
eat away the meat
free up the seed.

I'll be your guide,
coax the puckered
buds from your mouth,
buoy you up,
calm the heat at your core.

When you crack
your color will change.
Before your pulp
begins to glow
you'll be scarred.

I'll plant you in a sunny place,
feed you the powdered bones of fish,
warm your new roots with my hands,
wait for the fall,
when the harvest will be quickened by the rain.

THE NEW SOUND

Hordes of jackals cross the river,
Tame gazelles are grazing.
My eyes shiver in the shuffle.

I bull my way in the wake of beavers.
My mouth breathes
in the shadow of your breath.
My fingers
flank your hands.

I'm sorting the colors of whales.
I have you clowning and climbing the sky
floundering for a hand
to hold our sex.

In the poplar crows are calling
in the rain an orange
in my mouth the new sound of your unfailing tongue.

NORTH OF LAHAINA

for Trish Fox

The surf somersaults with the changing tide, tucked up and folded as if it were for that precise moment growing inside itself. A man and woman have entered their house to undress each other. The windows are open and the light is at their back. I lie down in the wet grass and watch as they begin to realize their bodies kissing inch by inch each by each. Their *talk* is the secret under the glass but I can read their palms as they lift out their private song. So I begin now, to hum too, these same notes, arranging and rearranging, passage after passage, improvising, bar after bar, even as they improvise, my nails ticking, mouth mimicking, weaving with my lips, my arms even, conducting our skin winding together pushing into the glass arching up from the lighted floor until my fingers fuse our blood, our very breathing, breath to breath.

AT MIDNIGHT

for Lyn and Mickey Freeman

She wakes to his
fingers turning
into the curves
of her face, his
fingers searching
through the hollows
under her eyes.

She feels too
his tongue licking
grain by grain, his
tears from her neck
where they'd dropped
like links of glass
hours before.

THE VISIT

You scale the canyons of my face
the bridge of my nose.
In the last light
you search
the mysterious crops
that wrap my head.

Tonight you will camp in my eyes
let in the sky.
As the moon goes green
you'll dig the trench
bury the stench of our breath
dam my blood
as it once burst over us
drowning all hope of escape.

(After a poem by Dylan Dow)

57

IV

BY DAWN'S EARLY LIGHT AT
120 MILES AN HOUR

BY DAWN'S EARLY LIGHT AT 120 MILES AN HOUR

for Gus Foster

1.

I remember the armless man at Riverview Park
rolling dice with his feet and writing poems in perfect script
with a pen he'd hold between his toes,
my friend Gene
            whose torso was propelled
                        in a chair
arms then
        so enormous and strong
he could walk
        upside down
for an entire block
        on his hands.

•••••

Who can rejoice in our strangeness!

Like the fish who lives
at 3000 feet
with no apparent source of light
creates its own light.

Like the two swordtails in the tank
both female   until
one orange and black tail just beginning
to pull
free
turns male
for the other.

•••••

Who *can* rejoice in our strangeness?

The peace that surfaces in a pint of gin
like trout feeding on flies
is seasonal . . .

How often we've stormed our stall
kicked out the old boards and stood triumphant
with no place to go . . .

The musk on the wind
shifts with the wind.
All we smell
these hot nights
is our own sweat
so we kick harder
spit back the shredded wood.

2.

On Tuesday morning
mouth stuffed with dried eggs,
eyeglasses crushed
at bottom of stairs
he scribbles on a doily
the tranquil face of a dancer
framed in curled auburn hair,
a terrified horse leaping
bales of burning straw,
a terrier balancing a multicolored rubber ball.

3.

As the surface of the earth at sunrise
gives up the naked body of a woman
you chase the road—coax

                        each
                  dial
            each
      meter
to perfect sync
100
      110
            120.
Only the rubber whines
only the wind . . . only
                        then you
trip the switch!

It is
      what
            it is
no second takes . . .

And so she is
as you found her
as you lifted her
so carefully
in your sure hands
and set her here
intact
that we might *trust* again,
learn to *see* again,
drink down the rain even—slowly
like the sycamore
a bit at a time.

*(After thoughts of Henri Toulouse-Lautrec and a Gus Foster
Photograph "By Dawn's Early Light @ 120 Miles Per Hour")*

EGG HUNTING

for Ted and Adrienne Overstreet

We climbed higher in the shale
the sweat leaking through our thick shirts
now and then kicking
chips from the edge — we'd
        watch them
    glide
down
to the river
at the bottom of the gorge.

•••••

We've been collecting these eggs for months,
sorting them
by size,
keeping them
warm,
hearing
their fine hearts
rustle under their skins.

The days are shorter
and the nights are cold.

We huddle in our robes
the eggs against our chests.

Today we ate our first
(a brown spore already growing over
the eye of the yolk).

•••••

We've gotten careless.
More and more shale
dribbles down
glistening in the sun
like opals
igniting the river,
scorching the gills of the fish.

•••••

The eggs diminish
the higher we climb.
At this altitude
the rocks have powdered,
the nests are dry.
Some young have hatched
they wrestle in the bag
some have died.

•••••

We lay out our lunch in a small hollow.
It's a lunch we've known before,
filled with the odors of dung
                    of coriander
                              of sperm.

We wring a neck,
pluck feathers,
eat a wing
and toss the rest over our shoulders
against the walls of the gorge
falling
end over end
pretending to fly.

•••••

Now the live ones are all eaten.
Only a trail of shells and bones . . .

We go to plant the last
the heart quit days ago.

We dig a hole with our bare hands.
He dances up
flapping his arms,
his tears
mocking his face. He
drives the fine, grey dust around us
churning up the echoes of wings,
of cracked shells
like gunshots.

We lunge
lock knuckles.
I can smell the river
(like my own sweat
like his breath against my mouth)
its silver skin
moving away
pulling
        slowly
                away
fifty thousand miles below.

RADAR

for Karin Epperlein

First
her suicide was first
something disallowed inside the heart.

She is young
has learned early
the art
of positioning her body
to manipulate her legs
walk on her hands
parade her naked hips
upside down
to make us partners.

•••••

My body wants to leap cartwheels flip
I decry pretense
will be irrevocably exposed
at one with the surf
only the moon to guide the tides.
I'll be drenched in sweat
and the sweet musk of the coconut
a juice as unique as my own.

•••••

Her sisters arrive
pass out knives
adjust their machines
connect the wires
load the guns
fill the rubber bags w/blood.

This is their solo
and I'm their witness
someone to hold the props.
When they plug in the wires
it's my signal to bleed.
I've learned to be brave
encourage them
it's been agreed.

•••••

I shower and rest.
Mother is upset.
She brings my robe.
I drink a cup of juice
joke with the horny stagehands.

I will die two more times tonight.
I do this willingly
watch the audience
flick my small wet tongue
entice
the real killers.

The last will be in water
dark as origins
where the dead
can drift
unscathed . . .

and who will come
to confirm
the doing

who will testify
it is done

and who will say
the strike was made
by them . . .

By water then
where great orange fish
pick
at eye
        or mouth
                or genital
where the corpse can settle
clean
and safe
white as any dream
born in your fetid air.

(*After a performance by:* SOON 3, San Francisco, CA, 1982)

SALMON

In Memoriam: Dennis O'Brien 1944–1980

As early as seven
I knew Salmon
would crawl between bark and trunk
in Spring
and become Willow
                    become
                              wild.

They were young then
their slim shadows gliding
under my perch
easing out on the fast water
going away.
But I could call their kind as they passed
SALMON.

By nine
I'd learned ten precious stones
to cook with the women
number pigeons in flight.

At twelve
I could run down rabbits
dig in the ground
as deep as the rest
sweat with the men.

August ended hot
the water high.
Salmon traps
were set again
wherever the river

bent around.
Sentries
were posted.

That night
I returned
to sleep
with The Willows.
At first light
was already
miles away.

My mouth toughened to a beak.
My skin was resplendent with long silver scales.
Behind me
        for miles
their now
        heavy bodies
slowly
      turning
the hot fish
ready to merge
SALMON.

I counted the nets and traps
counted the waiting
                  hands and eyes
signaled the first leap.

We slammed against the wood
dove into the nets
tearing them down
tearing it all
til the river was free
and we could stroke
unsheathed
        our gills

applauding
      each breath
our song
      resounding
boulder to boulder
its special chord
      reverberating
through the tangled roots
The Willows
      as we passed.

I leapt the last trap
past the eyes of the older men
gently nudging
the spent bodies,
my brothers and sisters already
fused to the dense spore.

I came to rest then
in my own time
willingly
on the slick round stones
in that mouth
where our first journey had begun.

Roger Aplon was born and raised in Chicago, Illinois. He began writing poetry in his early twenties at which time he was invited to join John Logan's highly regarded "Poetry Workshop" then attended by a varied group of what are now considered some of America's best young poets. In 1961, Aplon began editing CHOICE Magazine with John Logan and Aaron Siskind while continuing to publish his own work in numerous magazines. He is now living in San Francisco. His first book *Stiletto* was published in 1976 by Dryad Press and now he has given us this new collection of poems.

Designed and printed June 1983 in Santa Barbara for Dryad
Press by Mackintosh Typography. This edition is limited
to 1000 copies of which 150 have been hand bound in
boards and are signed by the poet.

Roger Aplon was born and raised in Chicago, Illinois. He began writing poetry in his early twenties at which time he was invited to join John Logan's highly regarded "Poetry Workshop" then attended by a varied group of what are now considered some of America's best young poets. In 1961, Aplon began editing CHOICE Magazine with John Logan and Aaron Siskind while continuing to publish his own work in numerous magazines. He is now living in San Francisco. His first book *Stiletto* was published in 1976 by Dryad Press and now he has given us this new collection of poems.

Designed and printed June 1983 in Santa Barbara for Dryad
Press by Mackintosh Typography. This edition is limited
to 1000 copies of which 150 have been hand bound in
boards and are signed by the poet.